Oct 30-72

Thanks
continuing supp...

Y0-CCO-251

Oeorgie

WORLDS WITHOUT END

Also by George Myers Jr.

Poetry
Angels in the Tiring House (1975)
An Amnesiac on the Verge of Heaven (1976)
Bodies of Water (1987)
Epiphanies: The Prose Poem Now, as editor (1987)

Prose
Nairobi (1978)
Natural History (1981, 1985)
An Introduction to Modern Times (1982)
Alphabets Sublime (1986)

WORLDS
WITHOUT
END

George Myers Jr.

Another Chicago Press

Acknowledgments: Many of these pieces first appeared in *Cotton Boll/The Atlanta Review, The Fiction Review, Fireweed, dialogue: arts in the midwest, Crazy River, Graham House Review, High Plains Literary Review, The Vincent Brothers Review, The Journal, Poet & Critic, Rampike, Coventry Reader, Nancy's Magazine, Contact II, River Styx,* and *The Columbus Dispatch. Seven Poems for the White Nile* appeared in *Nairobi* (White Ewe), and *Three Sonnets to a Mid-Western City* appeared in *An Amnesiac on the Verge of Heaven* (Fireweed).

The Kenneth Brecher quotations in "Multipurpose Stories: A Memoir With Postcards" are from *Too Sad to Sing: A Memoir With Postcards* (Harcourt Brace Jovanovich), copyright © 1988 by Kenneth Brecher.

"The Look of the World & Sometimes How It Feels" is in large part the result of John F. Wolfe, Luke Feck and David J. Baker having given me the opportunity to visit the People's Republic of China. To them, thanks. A different version of the journalistic sequence was published as "China Notebook: Sketches from the Land of Dragons" in *The Columbus Dispatch.* This new version is for Renmin Jim Breiner. The Chinese radicals in "Shanghai Rain," a translit of Guillaume Apollinaire's "Il pleut" (in turn, set by M. Pere), I've gleaned from the ancient Chinese almanac *T'ung Shu*; the others are from Edoardo Fazzioli's *Chinese Calligraphy.*

"New World Codex" is for my mother and father, who took me there. Bibliographic sources are William Bronk's *Vectors and Smoothable Curves*, Francis Robicsek and Donald M. Hales' *The Maya Book of the Dead*, William M. Ferguson and John Q. Royce's *Maya Ruins of Mexico*, Allan Schwartzman's *Street Art*, and Dennis Tedlock's translation of *Popol Voh: The Definitive Edition of the Mayan Book of the Dawn of Life and the Glories of Gods and Kings.*

"The World of the Book" is for Denny Griffith and Ann Marie Slaughter. "The Clarinetist Enters Heaven" is to the memory of Tom Myers. I'm indebted to Peter Balakian for "The Hills at Badaling," to Harrison Fisher for the Coleridge lines that begin "A Poem Beginning With a Sentence Dreamed by Coleridge"; and to Guy Davenport, Jerry Roscoe, Bob Fox, Taban Lo Liyong and Nancy Mairs.

Cover design by Scott Minister

Published in the United States of America by Another Chicago Press, Box 11223, Chicago, IL 60611.

This project is funded in part by generous grants from the Illinois Arts Council, the Ohio Arts Council and the National Endowment for the Arts.

Library of Congress Catalogue Card Number: 90-80551
ISBN: 0-929968-12-3 paper

FIRST PRINTING

Distributed by Independent Literary Publishers Association, Box 816, Oak Park, IL 60303.

Funded Through
Ohio Arts Council

Individual Artist
Fellowship Program

Contents

Outside
        outside myself
                there is a world
                — WCW, *Paterson*

The Book of the World

The vessel
of the world

is filled
by those who pour

it, and what comes
from it is theirs.

Open up   open out   open in

The Look of the World & Sometimes How It Feels

"The Tao that can be told is not the eternal Tao."
—Lao Tsu, *Tao Te Ching*
"I gave up the idea of its being illustrational;
I gave that up in China. It has to be put together
as one thing, text and images."
—David Hockney, on the making of *China Diary*

The Look of the World & Sometimes How It Feels

入

Jerrybuilt
partisans foot-step

over and under the poet
—outlaw, onus, ogre—

to get at the shambling
oviposited ode,

to carry Mao Zedong away.

見

They say the Great Wall of China, a meandering dragon of
gray ramparts and graffiti, is the world's largest cemetery—
its earthenware base corked with thousands of slaves who
died building it. They say we've just eaten kitten dumplings,
but we're told too late for us or it. They say there aren't
panhandlers here, but there are; and the residents of the gray,
squat shantytown structures are needy, indeed.

And they say you can't take riches with you, but China's
emperors tried. In one tomb, for example, more than 7,000
buried terra-cotta warriors and horses guard treasures and the
dead.

I am in one, two, three Chinas—one is strange, imperial
and gone. One is arbitrarily grim and mean, its aftereffects
evident in a generation of illiterates. The third is feverishly
green, smelling familiarly like capitalism. Swarming street
hucksters and spires of construction work are heard and seen
everywhere.

9

My ears and eyes are wide open, for tomorrow there may be four, five or six Chinas more. We are writers come to see a sampling of art objects once owned by China's elite and the all-powerful Sons of Heaven, China's emperors. Notebooks in tow, we shuffle into the court of the gold and crimson kings—into Beijing's Gugong Palace, an enclave surrounded by locust trees and narrow streets. Aspiring capitalists rush our bus to sell us sunglasses, cooked eggs and phony antiques.

We are escorted just inside the first wall of the Forbidden City, the famous city within a city where Ming and Qing emperors ruled. A youthful Yang Xiaoneng, wearing white gloves, carefully handles bronze vessels crafted 700 years before the birth of Christ. He gestures toward ancient bells, and porcelains, and the head and hands of a second-century B.C. jade suit intended to preserve the remains of a princess, Dou Wan. We're boiling, and the Chinese haven't broken a sweat.

雨

The far-off smash of an electrical storm
is frozen in a vase. The phonograph pours

out its *vous n'etes pas le seul.* Musicians
know the sound of old. With each rain

the drab leaves light up and start red
season's say. It sinks. It sways

that zebra of sleep: a dreamer's bouquet.
It's a tender country taking in green air.

I am not here.
I am not on the way.

10

廿

Beijing is befouled by coal ash and the dust blown off the northern steppe. The air is bad. Spitting seems nearly as common as breathing. Everything is unexpected. Not far from Mao's burial vault on the pompous acreage of Tiananmen Square, a kiosk offers Kentucky Fried Chicken and Pepsi. The Chinese, one-fourth of the world's people, are trying to climb back from Mao's catastrophic Cultural Revolution. During the revolution, from 1966 till Mao's death in 1976, the Middle Kingdom shut out the world, It embraced Mao's belief that a nation of peasants was a nation at its best.

Once powerful and feared, the Forbidden City was vilified as a horrible emblem of China's imperial past. Today it is a highlight of the burgeoning tourist trade. The dreamy headquarters of dynastic rule resembles Coleridge's "miracle of rare device, a sunny pleasure-dome." The palace looks like a garish jewelry box—five parts whimsy, five parts perfume. To enter is to peel back the skin of an onion.

Hands in Prayer

Fingertips are the common source
of sacrifice

prying the heart
from its very devotion

Beginning with a Sentence Dreamed By Coleridge

Varrius thus prophesied
vinegar at his door
by damned frigid tremblings.
Old Mao considers
(but no one follows. He once did)

11

the ersatz spring of his ersatz
ticker wound right as his golden watch.
An aide makes sure it goes
but no one follows. He once did

move, in a corporal way,
from one great distance to another.
"Just a matter of time." His time moves on
but no one follows. He once did.

示

We walk through Wumen, or the Meridian gate, the last
wall in China where a billboard-sized portrait of Mao still
hangs. Next, we cross a marble bridge to Taihemen, or the
Gate of Supreme Harmony. We are a few feet inside and an
unexpected world of imperial gold, saffron, yellow and
ochre, accented by tons of alabaster balustrades and
stairways, throws itself against us. The gaudy palace, a maze
of wood and yellow-glazed buildings and tiles, consists of
9,999 rooms and dozens of courtyards larger than football
fields. Nine was a holy number in imperial China, and
multiples of nine are found everywhere in and out of the city.
China's story is always told in numbers. The palace grounds
cover 260 acres; the ochre walls are 35 feet high. The inner
city dates to the 13th century, when the Yuan imperial house
was moved to Beijing.

It was Yongle the Ming who moved China's capital from
Nanking to Beijing and expanded the palace to its
Gargantuan size. Conscripts wrapped up work on the
wooden city in 1420, building it entirely of interlocking
joints—no nails. Curious schnauzer-like beasts adorn each
roof. The more totemic animals on the roofs, the holier the
building and what goes on inside. The palace had been
home to 24 Ming and Qing emperors. The last, the Manchu

emperor Pu Yi, was overthrown in 1911. The weak puppet-emperor abdicated a year later. For reasons commonly attributed to luck, rampaging Red Guards did not torch the Forbidden City during the Cultural Revolution. Ignited by Mao, militant youths at the time destroyed monuments to "the old way" throughout China.

In Imperial China, the despotic Son of Heaven handed out his brand of justice or made pronouncements from the Hall of Supreme Harmony. Guarded by ornate bronze lions, cranes and other symbols of his power or wisdom, the emperor sat amid cloisonne urns, miniature temples, incense burners, and a sundial and grain measure, twin emblems of justice. Carved into the ceiling above him, ascending dragons play catch with a ball called "the pearl of potentiality," representing the moon and good luck. Potential rose and set with the Son of Heaven. His word was law; his actions represented the moods of the gods. Because he was the gods' representative on earth, commoners could not look at him. *The public, the private, the public, the private.*

The dragon, a symbol of the emperor since the Han Dynasty, is unlike anything Beowulf or knights from Western fairy tales ever slew. It is scaly and snake-like but with feet and claws. It has a camel's head, the horns of a stag, the ears of an ox, rabbit eyes, a frog's belly, hawk claws and the palms of a tiger. These dragons can evaporate from sight, if they so desire, or shrink to the size of silkworms. A dragon can grow as large as the space between earth and heaven. It can't hear, but its voice resembles wind chimes. The mythical dragon, or *lung*, is benign, even friendly. It is easily frightened—especially by centipedes, or by swatches of silk dyed with five colors. Glass was thought to be a dragon's frozen breath, and cinnabar ore to be colored by its blood. The dragon traditionally rose in the east, with the sun, and from the direction of oncoming spring rains. Facing the dragon from the west is the white tiger, lord of death and darkness. The dragon rises to the heavens at spring equinox, shaking the dew or spring rains from its saw-toothed back before descending at autumn equinox. Emblematic of male vigor and fertility, it is yang to the empress's yin, symbolized

13

by the phoenix. The phoenix, or *fenghuang*, appears in folklore as a god of the winds at least 2,000 years before Christ. It was born in the sun and was said to sleep in a cave. The public, the private.

Outside the Hall of Supreme Harmony, down a marble walkway festooned with dragons, and in a courtyard big enough to accommodate 90,000 people, envoys arrayed in order of their rank would kowtow, hitting their heads nine times on the marble field as tribute to their liege. Some came to beg for their lives, or die, if it suited the Son of Heaven. Frequently it did. In the beginning, the great emperors were fierce warlords. At their zenith, they were peacemakers. In the end they were puppets, hardly the mighty rulers who unified warring states or built a wall stretching 1,500 miles.

‡ ‡

> "The louse suffers for the flea's misconduct."
> —Chinese proverb

We crowded in like so many black ants invading the home of a flea. But the flea once lived in the fur of his brother, a god. Our host is Pu Jie. He is short, even birdlike, his small hands pouring a bottle of tepid (we would discover) Ding Hu beer for a group of humidity-weary journalists. He sipped orange drink from a carton.

The end of his brother Pu Yi's Manchu rule began as soldiers led a mutiny in Wuchang on Oct. 10, 1911. Powerless, Pu Yi abdicated in February of the next year, his unlikely rise and fall the subject of *The Last Emperor*, Bernardo Bertolucci's epic film. But now, 20 of us, including our guide and two Party translators, crowded into Pu Jie's home. We listened as intently to Pu Jie's bright, clear voice as did accompanying officials from *The People's Daily*.

Pu Jie is accustomed to commanding attention, even in so humbly decorated a receiving area as his petite living room.

Pu Jie had seen *The Last Emperor* twice. Yes, he said, he liked it, and enjoyed seeing himself portrayed by an actor, though the scenes were short-lived. Then he smiled a quick, lambent smile, pushed his glasses up the bridge of his nose and said, "It wasn't exactly so, but that is to be expected in a movie."

Pu Yi had lived in the Forbidden City, a fortified baroque palace of egos. Pu Jie visited him frequently when a young boy. Pu Jie now lives in a studio apartment about 60 feet by 18 feet, large by post-imperial standards. The living room, half the size of his apartment, is decorated with small porcelain figurines and photographs of his late wife, his first granddaughter and of olden days in China and Japan. The modest flower-patterned tile floor is a far cry from the marble floors where he once played, where emperors stood.

Pu Jie's answers came easily. They sounded practiced. "After my brother abdicated," he said, "he tried to become emperor again but there was no support from the Chinese people." Pu Yi collaborated with the Japanese so they would "set him up as emperor in Manchuria. He was their puppet. He understood that."

When the Second World War ended, Pu Yi and his family were captured by the Russians in Japan and returned to China. "We thought we would be killed," said Pu Jie, "but we were spared. We were told we had a future here. China could have done what it wanted with us. It was hard for me at first. I was a Manchu. I had collaborated with the Japanese. I was used to being served. What was to be done with us? We were re-educated at a prison school and had to learn how to work. Pu Yi had it worse than me. He knew nothing about work."

Though Pu Yi's story was told to millions in celluloid, Pu Jie's is told to handfuls of listeners at a time, under the eyes of the Party.

"Before the empire was overthrown, I was a drop of dirty water in an ocean of clean people. Now I've merged into the clean water."

Pu Jie has lived in this apartment, walled off from Beijing's teeming streets by one of the country's many ashen gray walls. He said he comes and goes as a free man, and continues to work, "advising the government on a variety of things."

He stands to shake our hands. When we leave, Pu Jie will take out his brushes and ink and return to what he said was his favorite pastime, calligraphy. It was the hobby of emperors.

The Hills at Badaling

The hills
   rouge
      the sun

Pink and blue
   fresh
      like white

But take me
   in dust
      on the page

‡ ‡

The Great Wall at Badaling is China's version of our Niagara Falls. The view is emphatic; the trinkets, immaterial. Called the eighth wonder of the world, the Great Wall snakes from Jiayuguan Pass in central Asia to Shanhaiguan Pass by the Bohai Gulf. It is one of hundreds of wall fortifications stretching for hundreds of thousands of

16

miles, and it is their great gray primogenitor. Construction
began about 300 B.C., when leaders of warring kingdoms
had built parts of the bastion to hold back brigands from
neighboring states. In 221 B.C., Qin Shi Huangdi conquered
the states of Han, Zhou, Wei, Chu, Yan and Qi, ending 800
years of feudal wars and unifying China. From Qin's name
came China's.

Qin, a charismatic leader, was second to none in
exhibitions of imagination, toughness and villainy. Qin
standardized weights and measures, the length of cart axles,
clothing, the calendar, monetary units and taxes; and he
demolished existing, smaller walls between federal states to
forestall separatist movements against him. To keep peace
while he lived, Qin had his citizenry's weapons destroyed,
burned all books but those on medicine, astronomy and
farming, and beheaded or buried alive Confucian scholars.
He also made the most of slave labor, ordering 300,000
peasants and conscripts to fortify the Great Wall, and 700,000
more to build his mausoleum of terra-cotta soldiers. Each
warrior has a different face and supposedly was modeled after
members of Qin's army. A trench of more than 7,000 warriors
and horses, now under a huge hangar, has been unearthed
since the tomb was discovered in the Shaanzi Province, Qin's
old capital. *The public, the private.*

Qin's burial ground, a four-sided grassy pyramid
surrounded by souvenir salesmen, is unopened and believed
to be packed with treasures. On the top of his tomb,
pomegranate trees bloom. The nearby Mount Lishan resembles a wedding cake—terraced in layer after layer of misty
green icing interrupted only by the moving red dot of a
walker's hat, way into the distance. Qin's Great Wall is out
of view. In the 2,000 years since the first emperor, the wall,
also known as Wanli Changcheng or "the Wall of 10,000
Li," has been repaired and fortified countless times. The 600-
year-old stretch we hike along, the key North Pass of
Juyongguan Pass, was built by the Ming to protect Beijing
from raiding Mongols from the north. The lens cap to my
camera pops off and rolls 30 feet down a sharp incline. It
passes six Chinese tourists, who cautiously watch it roll past

17

them, before it bumps against a wall and halts. Almost 40 feet high and 20 feet wide at the top, the wall is big, yes, but too small to be seen from the moon, as legend claims.

Some 20 miles away at Juyong Pass is a 14th-century impediment to China's supernatural enemies. The Cloud Terrace, or Yuntai, is a stone and marble arch jammed with reliefs of ugly celestial guardians who hurl evil whammies at bad spirits, at everyone in six legible languages, including Mongolian, Uighurian, Tibetan and Sanskrit.

To the east is Qin's tomb and the neolithic village of Banpo, whose artifacts and trenches show how a matriarchal people lived 6,000 years ago. Shards of pottery, and corpses, many buried face down, are rudely displayed. North of Xi'an—once the grandest city in the world—are the burial chambers of 27 emperors. To the south are Buddhist temples and the great Tang Dynasty mosque, a mix of Chinese and Islamic architecture reflecting the influence of Japan and India and trade routes. And here is one of the world's oldest and largest encyclopedias, an eerie gray forest of stone tablets tall as three men. Calligraphy records of geography, geology, plant and animal life—the known history of men—are etched on 1,000 steles, many under glass or protected by roof. Beside and below the massive letterings are wee ones—ancient textual footnotes.

In Xi'an, carcasses of various beasts crawling with flies and streaming blood hang from hatrack-like meat hooks at an open-air butcher's shop. A little boy partly naked scoots away from my camera; his family members laugh and wave. A dozing man is perched on the lip of a wagon. Apart from the chunky stone Buddhas, he's the only Chinese we've found who would benefit from a diet.

Across this street is Xi'an Middle School No. 3, a complex of China-gray buildings built by British missionaries before the Revolution of 1949. By 500 parked bicycles, most of them Flying Pigeons built in Shanghai, exam schedules are posted on two weathered outdoor blackboards. The school's courtyard and buildings, in various stages of repair and disintegration, are in physical disarray but filled with smiling children. Within a few seconds, music blares from speakers propped in the yard's locust trees. It is recess. Children stream from their classrooms or hang from upper-story windows to look at me looking at them. Perhaps 100 of them fill the yard, and one student is pushed toward me. Her name is Zhang Li. She is 18, curious about my clothing and camera, and wants to come to the United States. Having learned English by first grade, she's a better diplomat than I am. I'm American enough to think I can learn Chinese in two weeks. We acknowledge my handicap and decide to speak in English.

She asks: "Is this your first time in China?" "Do you like it?" "Uh, Americans can choose their own studies, yes?" "If my marks are very high, I can go to a university, too." She said she'd go to any university in China, whichever would accept her. The music plays again, and Zhang and the others scamper back to their classes, Russian, English, chemistry and advanced algebra.

么

Lesson

The Buddhist monk Tripitaka and his three disciples were travelling to India for fetch Buddhist scriptures. On their way they met White Bone Demon.

The Demon caught the Tripitaka wishing to eat his meat and suck his blood for long life.

When the Demon played her trick the Monkey saw through it by his fire eyes and removed his golden staff to the Demon.

The Tripitaka wrongly blamed the Monkey for violating Buddhism law and drove him back to the Mountain of Fruit and Flowers.

After the Monkey went away, Tripitaka Pigsy and Sandy were caught and taken away to the Demon's cave. They in great danger. Pigsy asked Sandy to protact master himself

*fighting out the cave rushing to the Mountain of Fruit and
Flower asked the Monkey coming back for save the
Tripitaka.*

    *The Monkey came down his mountain pretending the
golden cicada went to the White Bone cave to attend a
banquet. In the hot oil pot the Monkey rolled three times.
The whole truth has come out and this Tripitaka very
regreted.*

    *The Monkey came to his true face with Pigsy. Sandy had a
heavy fight with the Demon. The Monkey spurting fire
burnt the Demon to dust.*

    *The Tripitaka and his three disciples continued on their
journey to India.*

水

Out Beyond the Kelp Bed

The wonder-world
hauls in its load

of lights, a liquid
cursive lapping

its name across our knees
answering our smallest hopes,

the little things.

    The chopsticks are no problem, but food can be a test.
Consider the sea slug in its charming repose. The purplish-
gray tubular thing is one of the dishes I'm served at a

banquet of imperial scope. If I don't put one of them on my plate—it quivers slightly when poked—my Chinese hosts will politely deposit two there.

With a mind of their own, my chopsticks propel a sea cucumber toward my mouth. I wish for a glass of one of those liquid "hair medicants" I see advertised, but wash the slug down with a warm beer. I did it. It's down.

I'm given something different to drink at a festival celebrating the Miao people. The Miao are one of China's 56 minority groups. The occasion is "an official welcome," a welcomed respite from the bus-tomb-bus grind arranged by our guides and *Renmin Ribao* or *People's Daily*, our Communist Party hosts. Singing to the screechy music of reed-pipe instruments called *Iusheng*, phalanxes of Miao women step toward us to pour down our throats—there's no getting away from it—mouthfuls of Maotai Jiu, or plain ol' Maotai. The Maotai is a determined little drink from the Miao people's native Guizhou. It's the color of hooves, comes in thimblefuls and goes away in about 12 hours. The Miao are extraordinarily handsome people, whose beauty is heightened by their bright costumes and baroque, horn-like headgear, said to symbolize the horns of their totemic animal, the water buffalo. Two acrobatic men jump through and around each other's legs, blowing horns all the while, dancing the "golden pheasant dance." I'm taken with the Miao and the Maotai isn't bad, either.

Decaying, elegant, cluttered Shanghai is yet another China. It is the world's fifth-largest city, with a population of more than 12 million. Once a center for the opium trade, then bombed and occupied by the Japanese from 1937 to 1945, the former "Paris of the Orient" is now a beehive of discos, department stores and boombox joints. Reflecting the citizens' alleged right to think and do for themselves, Zhu

Rongji tells *People's Daily*: "My creed is to think things out for myself." What sounds obvious and easy to us is brave here. (A headline in *The Beijing Review* refers to "mind emancipation.") Zhu is campaigning to be the city's mayor. It's hard to imagine this city as a hotbed of uprisings and political upheaval. During the Cultural Revolution, more than 500,000 leftists and scholars were expelled from here. *China Youth*, one of the country's many magazines, reports that self-employed young people want more knowledge and career advice, to expand "social contracts" and to participate in social activities. Just 11 percent want to become Party members.

Mr. Zhu unbound.
Mr. Zhu speaking, requiring
a certain space between words
between words
that seem
unreasonable

Finally divorced.
Finally says
"Not in things, but in ideas"
and finds the space, finds
fewer words,
lives in a gray house
in which he may or may not
be home for dinner tonight.

The waterfront Bund, a wide boulevard of 50-year-old buildings called Zhongshan Road, faces the stormy Huangpo River and East China Sea. The Bund is much-traveled but my cab driver, a Shanghai native, can't get me there. The street and directions on how best to get there are plainly written down for him in Chinese. But he grew up during the Cultural Revolution, missed an education and can't read. I try another cab. Cabbies rule the streets and navigate them with a wicked sense of humor.

Shanghai's 16th-century Yu Yuan Garden is a secret piece of paradise, like the Forbidden City, within a city. Flowers and persimmons blossom and raindrops bubble on fat leaves. Well-fed carp loll in a garden pool. Along the garden's high walls, black saw-toothed tails can be followed to dragon-head entablatures.

Rules are made to be followed even in old opium towns. At a crowded market in Old Town Shanghai, one of us is fined a few cents for dropping a match on a walkway over a lake. Twelve to 15 Chinese draw near to stare and eye the offender even 15 minutes after the policeman has moved on.

‡ ‡

Thinking of Apollinaire in a Shanghai Rain

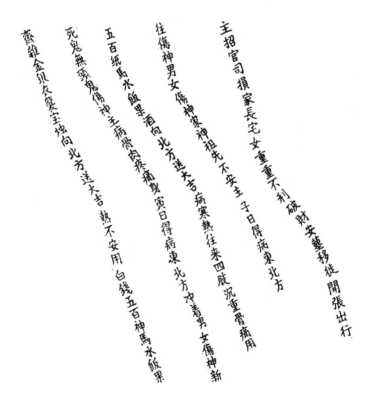

Waiting

Another oar in
the staring air.

    Along the lower reaches of the Qiantang River is the city
of Hangzhou and placid West Lake. Called Xihu in Chinese,
the lake is Edenic. Visiting in the 12th century, Marco Polo
called it paradise. It was famous then as now for its silk and
satin, and for foods its fine restaurants still offer: "Fish Head
with Soya Beancurd," "Cat's Ears" and "West Lake Fish in
Vinegar." The 4-mile-wide lake is surrounded by sienna-and-
ashen-gray pagodas, temples, tea gardens, green mountain-
sides of carved Buddhas, and caves slicked over by verdant
moss and rainwater runoff. Naming its highlights is to utter
secret charms: "Three Pools Mirroring the Moon," one of
them, is a man-made isle in a pond on a larger island.
Another is the Lingyin Temple, built in Xianhe's reign in
the Eastern Jin Dynasty in A.D. 326. here, inside the main
Buddha Hall, sits Sakyamuni, a giant golden Buddha carved
from camphor wood. Seated, he's 30 feet tall. Across from
him, nestled in cliffside caves, 300 Buddhas grin and laugh,
gorged on private jokes and happiness.

土

Rock. Bird. We are things.
Now all the stones have wings.

至

Three Fu dogs
jump from logs.

欠

We break our backs.
The day's intact.

Springtime in the Underworld

"The bee of the heart dives into it
and wants no other joy."
—Kabir
"A hive of questions. Each thought
its ration of honey. Bees. Bees."
—Edmond Jabes, *The Book of Dialogue*

Pluto in the Underworld

"Write, write, write in order to remember."
—Jabes

Lips, eyes, belly, arc of skin

I'm born without
all I'll ever know

the guy with a thesaurus
—planting Colorado pines
in the papaw patch.

Birds Wild at Night

"Unlike birds, books die with wings spread open."
—Jabes

The deer lapses   by the fire,
staring. A kind   of consequence,
           expelling   pale air.
           Black ducks stick
           on the lake. Flames
     want to be something, too.
Agitated, they leap and seethe. The spruce and fir stand
static as starlings and phoebes shoot about warily.
     Flames rear up, split wood into nickles,
     foil and flint. Each bird and animal
           exhales demented
           airs but we
           hold ours
           crazily

Pluto / Persephone

"I heard the footfall of the flower spring . . ."
—Sappho

What I believe in
now is desire

Now what in me
believes desire

What desire believes
in me is now

Now what
desire believes in me

Persephone, Swallowed Up in the Field

> "I wasn't kissing her, I was whispering in her mouth."
> —Chico Marx

The libidinous language,
the oola-oola
of the cunning
linguist, the musky air
of a hands-on experience—

The touch and go
of throat and below, the—

She drops into darkness

(Fragment) Beginning and Ending with Lines from Helene Cixous' Introduction to *The Stream of Life*

Generally, one holds back one's pleasure

There, in these moments,
is a kind of pleasure
of a pleasure

This is incapable of saying it
I want to
She knows it

One has to give oneself to that which gives itself

Persephone in Season

So, yeah, I met him
    I'm kinda *you know*
  I says *I wanna see*
    and he says *I've got what you want*
 Hey don't think I'm easy
    I'm imperial
   I work at it
    I kinda laugh
   He says
    I like chili heavy
  I could be ready
    put up my hair
    combed it out

   We walked
    my heel or something
   He seemed
    We were
   I heard
    possess
  that was it
    placed in the universal blueprint

   He smiles
    thinking he understands
  every turn
    Everything plays, as we choose
  to be open
    to innocence and its opposite
We love in each anyhow
    So, yeah, I met him

  He takes me, see
    He wanted some things from
    Sears, too
  and I says
Hey I got my own things here, you wanna look?

34

I grabbed some
        Hey, I can tell what people got
        just by looking
He's saying *yeah oh yes*
        darting like a bee

He insisted that we met
        He leaned in slow
    said
        lips
    I was ready
        Man, gimme what you got

    He moved
        This opening
   Everything wet
        I'm hiking it up
  A little drink?
        Something euphoric, I think
  I wasn't neglected
        How lucky for him
    Nearer, then
        down goes the strap
 We were making
        pink
that's it, *pink* sounds
        silky
        absolutely
        stuff like that
 my green legs wide

    Madly
        but nervous, aware that
  life was against
        the only
 mover he ever knew
        —*winter*

We lay in the pool of ourselves

        He paused
                to rub
       I'll say
              he got tense

     Loved a good fight
              lay
         get off
             I mean *steam*

I've had a piece
  let it ride
I'm hurt
  I eat the pomegranate
If not that
  then something else
He could kill for it once a week

     Where there's tinder
                flare-ups sear whatever's in sight
      Well *you do me*
           I told him back
           ....

It cost me opportunity, going down there

Not chances, but opportunity, reprisals

  Okay
    I'm not going to tell
           won't give you
   So I'm going to insist
          He knew me a bit
    but he wasn't ready
         not for people
         not steady anyway

what does he do but
thrusts his hands in his pockets and he walks outside
             get that, outside
                         he goes outside
outside and waits for something to happen

I'm happening I'm telling him
Look at what I got for you

but he's out walking his big estate

He's a big dope, resourceful
    but a dope
His big thing? He can't stand green
So, shit, I'm outta there, back in time for spring

The Further Adventures of Pluto

Unafraid to have a piece
of the action
     if only
this poem

(Poem) Found Burrowing in Nabokov's
Ada or Ardor: A Family Chronicle

Master, Our Likenesses Endure

.

Making Out; Letting Enter

.

Morgan, Observe, Loathes Endings

.

Mygod, Other Lips Embracing

.

Me, Oh Lord, Envious

.

Magically Observing Life's Echoes

Pluto's Nocturnal Palindrome

Too hot to hoot, so remain a mere man. I am Eros.

Demeter's Anagram on This Love Business

Compensations
pass coin to men.

Zeus Casts Pluto and Persephone as Postmoderns

She fits her shelf
with intrigue's Top Ten.
She leans to flowers, hates

what she has a fondness
for, knows who and why.
That's that. He speaks

of dryness, the world's end
and has a certain charm.
He sleeps in spectralwear

anytime, anywhere.
The pricking of stars
stares them down. They move

closer, crablike, if that's close,
talking the boundary talk,
the endless loop of language.

Their rippling arms
and legs will toast the air.
Small dewlips of sweat

from past vetos will fall
the length of gravity.
She promises, or he does.

They'll think it over.

**(Passage) Opening into Three Lines
from Stein's *Tender Buttons***

Is there pleasure
Is there pleasure   there

Is there pleasure there
There is

Is there pleasure when
There is

When there is

*Is there pleasure when
there is a passage, there
is when every room is open*

New World Codex

"To see ourselves, should we look at each other?"
—William Bronk

". . . let us retrieve the lost letter or the
obliterated sign, let us recompose the dissonant
scale, and we will become strong in the world of
the spirits."
—Gerard de Nerval

Stela 1

This is the beginning of the ancient word,
Facing the faces   in the
vine-split wall, an invisible time
left visible
based on a year of 260 days   formed by
joining the day-names   to their numbers
Mayan time   before times
of simply walking from one place to places
where there was   no times
20 days meant a uinal   18 uinals
were called a tun   20 tuns
a katun   A word meant 23,040,000,000 days
here in this place called Quiche. Here we

Stela 2

shall inscribe, we shall implant the Ancient
underworld, that of death   represented
in the events   of the day, the numbers
of the days named for their gods   rooted
in the upper world through which door will
open allegorically   to start
to begin   to open
the jaws   of the
monster   God K
falling   into
the setting   sun
the motion   on
Word, the potential and source for everything

Stela 3

done in the citadel of Quiche, in the nation
of stela, granite slabs   decoded
by generations ahead,   coded
by them   for the Nunnery
the Mask Tower the Venus Temple and Dovecote
of Uxmal, Palenque, Kabah, Zlapak, Coba and
Chichen Itza, Tulum, Sayil, Labna   places
from 3,000 BC   the start
of a flowering   gone
but to where?   To time
vegetation, tourism   places
from those born in the   brought-out, lights
of Quiche people. And here we shall take up

Stela 4

the demonstration,   *revelation*
by the Maker   Begetter
Tapir, Plumed Serpent   Coyote
Heart of the Lake, Heart of the Sea   the
Maker of the Blue-Green Plate,   defenders
Maker of the Blue Green Bowl   whatever
no matter   name it what will
It doesn't matter but   to those without
First it is first and last a book   A book
A book, a language record   of
Jaguar Quitze, Jaguar Night, Mahucutah   and
True Jaguar   all strength
and account of how things were put in shadow

48

Stela 5

and brought to light. There are generations
They were decoyed
but our birds just got hung up in a tree
we'll just turn their very being around
the anger in their hearts came down upon
their own heads
stretching the cord on the sky
pulling it that it might rain
for rain gave way to growth
and growth gave way to jungles and
those jungles did move to eat the
very buildings, all that was left
in the world, there are country people, whose

Stela 6

faces we do not see, who have no homes they
Palenque was abandoned   and the Great
Ball Court at Chichen Itza   the largest
in Mesoamerica 545 feet by 225 feet, target
rings 20 feet into the air, slanting mostly
outward, built just before the Toltec fall,
collapse, built for ostentation because the
Mayan, the New Mayan here, were   foreign
and self-conscious, where   a ball
hard, rubber   was to be spiked
through the hollow part, now especially the
empty place   emptied
wander through very small and large woodlands

Stela 7

"And for the Mayan civilization, everywhere was outpost."
—Bronk

like crazy people. And all the tribes were
"It's just a skull."   In the Chichen
Itza Ball Court the players wear kilts and
yokes   curling smoke
from mouths   a play has been beheaded
from his neck emerges   serpents
a squash vine everything   alive again
the head clattering, twisting   all over
the court, out of the court's gray cracked
walls through sun-bleached terraces plazas
toward the river, into the river   rivers
leading   finally everywhere
happy when they saw there weren't many of them.

Stela 8

It was said that these were enough to keep
The Nunnery Annex: Looking again to
the main structure, one sees now
how it was changed, modified
by the Maya-Mexicans (the Maya
period ended in the ninth century).
The great gash on the building's right
side, by the original chacmool, is where
Augustus Le Plongeon (1826-1908)
dynamited his way into the Monjas core,
finding the inner structure,
now ruined
them mindful of what was in shadow and what

Stela 9

was dawning. And all the tribes plotted again:
The nine lords of the Cauecs
The nine lords of the Greathouses
The four lords of the Lord Quiches
"How are we going to beat them?"
They were just making talk, all of them.
The two lords of the Zaquics
Great Toastmaster of the Reception House
Lord Crier to the People
Lord Minister
Four lords led the Lord Quiches, with their
palaces ranged around
And now is the joining together of the tribes.

Stela 10

They knew whether war would occur;
Bird House
Black Road
The Blame Is Ours
Blood Gatherer
Blood River
Blood Woman
Bloody Teeth, Bloody Claws
Bone Flute, Bird Whistle
Bone Sceptor
Bracelet of Rattling Snail Shells
Broken Place, Bitter Water Place
Everything they saw was clear to them.

Stela 11

"Do not reveal us to the tribes when they search
The guide takes a splinter of straw, holds it up
to those of us in his group. He is Mayan, he says,
and makes a trick with the straw. It is something
that we don't explain right later.
It is told like this:
There was a Mayan who built a thing
and it outlasted him
and the jungle grew over most of it
and it still is mostly hidden.
Now he comes back, once a year,
and makes it for the ones that come next.
for us. They are truly numerous now. They belong

Stela 12

to us.
    "The scene on Vessel 90 is static; it shows
three dignitaries adjacent to the now well-known
complex of codex, round bundle, bloodletter and
shell; to which in this scene an elaborate
helmet has been added. Again, it is likely that
these paraphernalia are being prepared for
transportation."
                    —Francis Robicsek, Donald Hales
    The Maya Book of the Dead: The Ceramic Codex
A model to compose
a codex
using ceramic vessels as pages

Stela 13

Although you were destined to join the dead
Here, in an uncomplicated spot,   hot
arid even   cooler   at hotel
to gather up all the information one can be
sure about   not purpose not
swarms of yellow jackets or wasps   not
our heart or pork or drinks or hands
only the smoke of Copal
its trail
from the Macaw House
the lesser
next to the great Seahouse
you will not because there is another time

Stela 14

ahead where our grandfathers, our fathers
XXXXXXXXXX   XXXXXXXXXX
XXXXXXXXXX   XXXXXXXXXX
XXXXXX   XXXXXX
XXXXXX   XXXXXX
XXXXXXXXXX   XXXXXXXXXX
XXXXXXXXXX   XXXXXXXXXX
XXXXXXXXXX   XXXXXXXXXX
XXXXXXXXXX   XXXXXXXXXX
XXXXXXXXXX   XXXXXXXXXX
XXXXXXXXXX   XXXXXXXXXX
XXXXXXXXXX   XXXXXXXXXX
had their sowing, their dawning.

Stela 15

And Jaguar Quitze, Jaguar Night, Mahucatah and True
                    Copal incense
                    Actually spoke
                    Staple foods
                    Flesh of
                            sweet things, thick
                    with yellow corn, white corn,
                    and thick with pataxte and cacao
                    countless zapotes, anonas, jocotes,
                    nances, matasanos—the rich foods
                    filling up the citadel, the place
                    shown by animals.
Jaguar were overjoyed when they saw the daybringer.

Stela 16

And these are the names of the animals
                    the walls were not all
easy to read   some cracked
fallen apart   maps of misreading
leverage lost to water, air and time
chunks, pieces
                    ground off for paste
out in the clear light a message comes
want it or not
          Makers or Modelers
                            you
You!
who brought the food: fox, coyote, parrot,

54

Stela 17

crow. There were four animals who brought
"When it's hand-hewn and looks like art,
it would either be as truthful a portrait
as possible (John Ahearn's casts), or made
of recycled debris, as are David Wells'
deer-and-hunter sculptures, cut from old
poster-clad plywood fences and then situated
in open lots. According to him, 'I wanted to
make something about the landscape, what's
built on it, what was once there, and how
people experience it now not knowing about
how it was experienced before.' "
the news of the ears of yellow, white corn

Stela 18

But their faces did not die; they passed
—Allan Schwartzman's
  Street Art
Layers upon layers
upon layers upon
layers upon layers
Stories
Lodging
Hands hidden
a collection
stone pages, postscripts
Waters of
them on. Here is the name of their citadel.

Stela 19

The first thing tourists do is find a place
under an arch, placing themselves in a
building or palace, framing themselves
for a photo.
Then they walk out, across a long
terrace, perhaps, or up a hill in
the fierce sunlight, and stand in
another building or under another arch
and have their photo taken there, too.
Then they get back in their trucks
and drive back to Merida
where they have their photos taken in hotels.
Then they put their photos in a book.

Stela 20

Then the book is shown to family and friends.
Sometimes it is kept for a long, long time.
It may be forgotten, eventually.
And then it will be remembered
found in an attic chest   hidden
away for months, decades, years   lost
and then discovered   perhaps children
motivated   without regard,
much to do   it is found
first   by one and
then   less hurriedly
by many   traveling
in from another time

World Premieres

"Every force evolves a form."
—Mother Ann Lee

The Secret House

of the toothpaste
is chalk, water, paint,
seaweed, anti-freeze, paraffin,
detergent and peppermint. Think

of it as you read your newspaper
— hemp, linen, wool, asbestos,
glass fibres, glues, loose ink —
or walk across the broadloom

of electricity, sucking in
400 volts, discharging
the moment you touch the knob,
the very moment too soon. Think

of the dead cells oozing out
giant ropes we'd rather call
hair, the bending hangers upstairs
giving off low-frequency moans

of despair. Think of it, them, you, it
: the microscopic wars, the webbing
of oxygen curling out from walls,

of things that happen without you,
behind your back, without any luck at all.

Brave New World

Conkles Hollow, Ohio

Rock split
along pre-existent trails
weakest at their vertebra, across veins
balanced by the globe
of a raccoon's skull,
of a still-legless salamander.
Tapped by a faint beat,
it reports the halves
of death ending
and death beginning.

We are first exposed
where last we commingled:
I hold this thing

in my palm,
it unfolding
lifetimes away,
like the foremost
inseparable
embryo.

Where Worlds Collide

Length by inches, temperature by degrees,
minute by minute. The unit of light
flux is the lumen, 12 candles in
12 directions every hour on
the hour. Here, let me
explain: On the
_____

surface of the
book, a road, your
hand, we find illumination
every second. To see this you need
15 footcandles per icicle, per spray of
water in rainbow glass. You'll get it after a time.
REFLECTED   REFRACTED
LIGHT   LIGHT

Multipurpose Stories: A Memoir with Postcards

1.

Ambience irks him. Lyceums peeve quite too much.
Twentieth-century music, black paintings, rubber sculptures
and the worrisome feeling that his eclecticism is slipping
bothers him rather badly. He long ago should have begun
writing realistic, necessary books about trout fishing, Slavic
dinners and carpenters or, frankly, journalism. He fears his
critics saying, "My God! He's shrinking fast! He's reached
the *Collected Essays* stage at last! Now comes the piss." But
what can he do? He once knew Alger Hiss.

2.

His father moves the suitcases from the garage into a U-
Haul. He finds one or two crates in the closet and puts them
in the truck, too. The family album is face down on a chair.
Someone asks him if he can find a cab. He says, "Yes, I can
find a cab. That at least is not a problem." The last time you
saw him he was unpacking some of your old clothes from a
trunk. The breeze made them move like a manta ray. It
moved toward you.

3.

She's depressed. It could have been anything, really. She
daydreams of black suicide. In her mind, she stands beside
herself and with a small hand gun fires a clear path through
her body, several paths in fact, from front to back, like little
plum lines. Little fountains of water erupted from the holes
and water swept over her like lilacs across a gazebo or a lawn
memorial, pleasing her, or did they?

4.

"He that loves me most, wounds me."
—Gambara

Debussy, in a letter describing *Le Martyre*, wrote: "I
needn't tell you that the worship of Adonis is mingled in this
work with the love of Christ."
Sebastian demands that Marc and Marcelian renounce
their faith, *as he must do*, but encourages them to remain
steadfast in their belief by converting their mother
    and loving that which he could love
    by moving in a secret place
    and opening a secret heart

‡ ‡

Bronze doors open to a blinding nova,
a satellite, lit celery aflame
illumined, on fire

Suddenly that day will never be the same

giving to new rule

A common source
   of duration
     and sacrifice

from brevity
   to vulgarity
     —a way out

of time
   a heart's devotion
     crowned by a common

63

form, the very forces
  that bring deception
    and punishment

that fulcrum
as its vessel

‡ ‡

"The slings and arrows. . ."

When his archers rescue Sebastian from
suffocation, they are commanded to bind him
to a tree and execute him with their own
arrows. (A history)

"Who loves me best shoots straightest,"
he tells his men, a perfect shot at bliss.
(A history)

A Vessel, a body possessed by arrows,
  is carried off

The arrows vanish, a mossy work done
  by scores of orchestras

They reappear, aflame, in a tree
  that held his hollied head

Unbound, aglow and more luminous
  lighting up the forest

A gigantic lily driven from the shoals
  leaking saxifrage, abounds

"Something wonderful and something terrible happened to me when I went to Paris." Kenneth Brecher, in Paris to do some sort of research on museums, goes on to say that the two most important women in his life died within months of one another. Alone, exhausted from grief, he began to wander the City of Lights, buying postcards where he went and adding them to the collection he began as a child. "I read all the time and looked at my postcards."

Brecher had been a collector since studying at Oxford, since living with a tribe of Amazonian Indians in Brazil, since seeing where the Blue Nile met the White Nile in Khartoum, and since climbing the Himalayas in Ladakh. His retained postcards, not mere mementos, were a world to him, and he sought solace through them.

"Postcards can be amiable as well as profound," he says. "Postcards can be dangerous: They can alter your life. They may even on occasion offer intimations of how we should live our lives."

He began thinking about his cards in a metaphysical sense, culling them into artifacts of an import greater than the tourist-shop variety. To him, they became iconographic, symbolic of all the people and phases in his life. He published his musings, and many of his cards, in *Too Sad to Sing: A Memoir with Postcards*. It is a toss-up as to whether his text or images interest more because Brecher's soliloquy soars, and his ability to be an archivist of the curious—of the grotesque, of the funny, of the beautiful—is amply represented in his postcards.

"These cards," he writes, "have an extraordinary power for me. Practically every time I look at them I understand a little more about myself. They serve as a private record, a means of measuring change, not unlike the marks on the kitchen wall that record a child's height. It has never been the religious iconography in itself that interested me. Most often it is a detail, like the thorns of the lilies, that transcend the image and feeds my hunger for metaphors and symbols that comment on the human condition. By noting what affects

me most each time I look at these cards, I find that I can get
some perspective on my own life."

In his final chapter he lists those qualities of a postcard
that would make him want to possess it. It would be a card
"that bears the likeness of someone very much like myself
and has this legend on the back: 'Do not be deceived by the
sadness in this young man's face. He is just beginning to
understand that what dies with him is precisely what is now
there to sustain him.'"

6.

Rome: Dear Editor, As you requested, here's
a poem with both "ore" and "pomeranian" in it.
And my contributor's note: I did not recently
win the Orlowsky prize, given annually to the author
of an original contribution to the study
and understanding of the visual arts published
during the preceding year in the English language.
My favorite sound is the dry cough of a .45
from an arid basement in Rome. It's time for juice.
Away with the manger. I and my friends are fools.

Middletown: Dear Editor, if ever a city could have
a horoscope, this is the one. Wedding and hanging
is destiny, it would say. I give up. I can't compete
with the future. Sometimes I dream I'm in another
country, a country of fortune cookies,
beef burgundy and ravioli. The Sundance Kid
(a stutterer like me) once fell asleep
on a map and dreamed of another country.
A sheriff there said, "Live or die but end
your sentence." Dreaming, I began to interpret
his dream and, finding no key, dreamed I never
awoke. I exchanged mail with this or that dream.

7.

Don't send a poem to do a paragraph's job. I accept all
your presents except the last. His joy was in excess, at the
news of his access to fortune. Though your terms exceed my
expectations, I must accede to them. Idiots are harbingers of
good luck; their innocence causes them to be led or directed
involuntarily by unseen powers. The best cosmetic is air and
exercise. He pretended to exorcise evil spirits. Both assent to
go up the ascent. He was indicted for indicting a false letter.
Champagne is made in France. The soldiers crossed the
champaign. If the palm of your right hand itches, money
will come your way. The law will levy a tax to build a levee.
The levee was held at the mayor's residence. The senior
brother was addressed as Senor. I don't have time for
breakfast; I only have time for cake. Air, for me, for all its
plenitude, is space.

8.

Words properly accented on the second syllable include
trustee, monsoon, prolix, gainsay, adept, romance, odeum
and philippic, which this is not.

Lake Effect Palindrome

$$\frac{\text{Ebb, be.}}{\text{No word, no bond, row on.}}$$

Ebb, be.

Sestina for Its Sleeper

Our bodies were a field
We saw the sun swell up like a river
The heat did not move
Sky moved over its sleeper
Insects hung in the air
Green and gold leaves faded in light

We saw the sun did not move
Heat moved over its sleeper
The sky hung in the air
Insects faded in the light
Green and gold leaves were a field
Our bodies swelled up like a river

Heat hung in the air
The sky faded in light
Insects were a field
Green and gold leaves swelled up like a river
Our bodies did not move
We saw the sun move over its sleeper

The sky was a field
Insects swelled up like a river
Green and gold leaves did not move
Our bodies moved over the sleeper
We saw the sun hang in the air
Heat faded in light

Insects did not move
Green and gold leaves moved over the sleeper
Our bodies hung in the air
We saw the sun fade in the light
The heat was a field
Sky swelled up like a river

Green and gold leaves hung in the air
Our bodies faded in the light
We saw the sun in a field
Heat swelled up like a river
The sky did not move
Insects moved over the sleeper

Solitude

Solo
etude

Outbursts After the Armory Show

"Prends l'eloquence et tords-lui son cou."
—Paul Verlaine

There is no future for the pastoral
as a literary form!

Warning! The authentic!

With trees
like delicate quilts,
with boughs, brown and green,
with sweet clover,
in her mouth is memory

.

My sweetheart will bake me a loaf and I'll cherish it,
watching the rockets lean down for a last look. The sky is
hung low with milk. The cat is buried in the leaves. Captain
Johnny recalls his sermon, wondering what's new in New-
castle. The horse is exploded in the road. The war rains
down. My grandfather, deaf, sucks yellow gas in a trench.

.

Under above, I forget
the nature of a crow flying
against the wind

breaking in on rhythm

to silence, to conceal
that which drums
the doughboy's beat.

Sound off. One two.
Naked or dead,
shall we descend the staircase?

Four Quatrains Ending With a Letter
of the Alphabet as the Flight
of a Marsh Hawk

". . . wonder takes all forms. . ."
—Ronald Johnson

a / b / a / b
a / b / b / a
a / a / a / a
a / a / x / a

UUUUUUU

Three Sonnets to a Midwestern City

Modern Forte

1.
It is night. A small fox has been tucked underneath
your pillow as a reminder. Edna St. Vincent Millay
is dead. Poems are crumpled in corners, black
notebooks, mason-ware jars with yesterday's
white carnation still good. The house hums
with unsoft singings of *I've got murder in my heart
for the judge.* The window ledge grows scales.
The breeze tastes like tar. Do you smoke now?
When you walked away your arms went out and your legs
went out and your face went out. It was like a foxtrot.
What was left behind: carnation, lampshade, jars.
The Nazis made lampshades out of skin; they were popular.
Yours is leaves picked from fall. You rolled over
and clicked off the light. I remember nothing went out.

2.
I'm very happy. Tell me something good. I have never
seen the interior of the pantheon, Rome.
Phone bills are annoying. *My period is overdue.*
I met the nicest guy today, he's really fantastic.
The most sensible thing about poetry is that it
is rarely confined, unless perhaps by itself.
Mayan shamans sing their dreams, bend over
backward to please anyone watching.
There's one thing we can learn from this
: Beauty mistakes itself for love. O how I'd love
to stab the sonnet. *I met the most wonderful
boy and girl today. You'll just love them.
This thing with you and me is over.* Oh.
Oh, I said. Oh. Some leave sawdust. Some, bones.

3.
Food, water, safety and a place to raise
their young: Animal mythologies, bestiaries
are worth noting. "I doubt if there is anything
in the world uglier than a Midwestern city."
: Frank Lloyd Wright, August 1954. I still think
about animals in these damn ugly towns.
I don't read Edna anymore.
Faces are set against the moon each winter.
It's a season one gets to know.
In winter, Celtic druids used mistletoe
in fertility and regeneration rites.
My hair is getting thinner.
Animals never say when.
They just go away.

Ice Cream

From the cone
to your lips

into my mouth
forever

Seven Poems for the White Nile

1. Into alpha,
   the resurrected men
   lighten their loads
   on the river's back

2. (   )

3. Along the shoreline,
   where the seams of the heart
   make the Rift Valley expand
   (this is a long way)
   but watch the foliage
      Lazy crocodile in dust
         You didn't think I was
         watching you so intently

4. East current through
   the acacia—

      Waterbuck
         the rare abandon

5. The world's pearl puts a gleam
   in our eyes (the insects)
      Take off your coat
      Let us see you

6. The bend—a lone Turkana
   Please water

   Child on her mother's back
   The current

7. Thin needle blood
   of a river flowing

The Clarinetist Enters Heaven

"Between geological matter and air, there is the shared surface."
—Michel Leiris, *Brisées*

Two lines of sound
                    from a bell
        nearly touching,
                    preparing to cross
            over, leaving
                    behind circumstances
            —the caprice
                    of separate lives
        that, at the last
                    endless difficulty,
        much too finally
                    come together.

2.

        Two lines,
                    not wide apart,
        unknowingly
                    to you, trilling,
            timing the
                    disclosure
        of pleasure,
                    stinging
            carefully,
                    delicately,
            audible
                    at last.

3.

Mouth the reed
              to bend the arc
       that rends,
              to drive apart
       the whole,
              as in geometry

4.

It goes toward
              some paradise or dell,
       the music
              lento, not strong,
and now less so

              There he goes
       blowing out
              the candle,

his lofty note too, too exact

How the World Came To Be

"O landless void, O skyless void
O nebulous, purposeless space,
Eternal and timeless,
Become the world, extend!"
—Tahitian creation tale

"What a lovely day again!
were it a new-made world"
—Herman Melville, *Moby-Dick*

"Mumbo-Jumbo is dead in the jungle."
—Vachel Lindsay

The World of the Book

After Mallarmé's *Le Vivre, instrument spirituel*

1.

The alphabet: I live in the crest of a C, smack in the belly
of a hammocked glyph. Above me, the overhang; beside me,
the sloped acclivity; at eye level, an open window to my life's
sentence, which spreads out now ahead of me. Cautiously, it
says: Take, eat, make, print. May I, can we, must we, when?

The Book is all, everything.
Everything is a page from The Book.
A word from The Book is a world, which itself is shelf to
innumerable books.

2.

Modello, sketch, opening: The Book (that is, the artist's
book) is an activity, what Robert Darnon calls a "construal
of meaning." As with all of literature, The Book is a reading,
a verb, and not a canon. Everything should be possible with
The Book. Who said a book about 20th-century art could
never be typeset in Baskerville, and why?

3.

Indirect lighting: The margin is a zone, too.

4.

Art history: The 1988 reprinting of *The Book of Kells* was
done to make available, once more, the 11th-century gospel's
exquisite color illustrations. In one, an elaborate *"I,"* like an
erect tongue, sticks up at God. In another, blue quails
rendezvous with dervishes, and sentences break into green-
and-red lynxes snorting fire. But the unfinished *Kells* is as
incomplete as our understanding of it. It is only a trace.

Quiet now. This is a secret.

This is a clement dream.

Come closer. *Shhhh*, this is a manifesto.

While looking, we possess a sense of apperception, and feel our thoughts about what we see assimilated into the foolscap. It happens without effort.

5.

Context, dye transfer: Is it inappropriate to intersperse pages of Margot Lovejoy's *Postmodern Currents* (1989) with pages from the 1948 fairy tale, *The Little Lame Prince?* And what if both become more clear that way?

We feel recognized by that which looks back at us. It feels a bit strange but, no, it's no trouble. We can close up The Book with the ease with which we rouse ourselves from a terrible or lovely dream.

6.

Art criticism: Fully half of The Books produced in the last decade focus on the virtuosos who produced them. Antonio Porcha said we "tear life out of life to use it for looking at itself." What a terrible shrinkage in subject matter, and a debasement of the contingencies of collage. This self-script is too much like the weary newspaper columnist producing 20 inches of "news" each day. Says novelist Gilbert Sorrentino, "Writers who arrange their lives so as to 'have experiences' in order to reduce them to contemptible linguistic recordings of these experiences are beneath contempt." But I can't decide: Isn't it the collector, and not his souvenir, which is ultimately more exotic?

Once seen, forever envisioned.

7.

Decorum vs. dry mounting: The subject must fit its
wanting; The Book must take its shape. Education and language go hand in hand; eroticism and language go tongue in
groove.

One must play. Or get out of the way.

8.

Technique, shapes, poetry: In The Book, the line,
especially the line break, needs rescuing from academe. The
craftsmanship we often honor in respect for tradition can
reinforce a cultural hierarchy, a country-club culture, to
which certain kinds of writings (that is, certain writers) need
not apply. Using the line specifically as a political
synecdoche, the critic James Scully argues for art forms that
actively oppose exclusionary power structures. "In the
province of 'culture,' we're overridden by poststructuralist
theories and postmodernist avant-gardes, regardless of political profession, speaking a uniformly muffled language
behind one or another institutional wall. A wall that, though
not opaque, is socially concrete."
Attempts to pull down the "monumental pieties of bour-
geois humanism," he says in *Line Break: Poetry as Social
Discourse*, too often are entrusted to respectable butler-types
who keep the lid on class and racial exploitation. Fact is, as a
system of set responses to a creative dilemma, as a preset
judgment, technique usually works *against* content. Scully
believes line breaks should be viewed as unconstrained "areas
of engagement," not boundaries. A fully realized poetry will
demystify language and the rules that the praetorian
academy use to govern it. While particular examples of that
kind of poetry may be found, it is doubtful the current cultural hierarchy welcomes them. Look around; what kinds of
writing do you see most?

9

Verso: (vúr so) n.; a left-hand page of a book or manuscript, opposed to *recto*. One must speak the other's language. Like, a lid off a daffodil, reading the same way forward and back. As in: so many dynamos. Is there ever a place where a page doesn't face another?

Mimetic books about non-mimetic images do not invite each other to the same parties. They invite discourse, not action; they seek to explain, not to show or compel. Such books remind me of Nicolas Calas' comment: "When language becomes prosaic, poetry ceases to exist."
The preceding paragraph, then, no longer exists.

10.

Close readings: The Book's middle name is *oo*. Do we want to know it well enough to know that?

11.

Lyre, lyre: One of Keith Smith's bookworks is a string book, one of his signature pieces about light and shadows. The artist's page compositions are altered by the shadows worming across the pages (the fields) of play. The string is three-dimensional type—sans serif, I'd guess. How many ways can you read his book? In more or fewer ways than *The Little Lame Prince*, and why?

12.

Technology vs. democracy: Technologic changes never made The Book less expensive. But it did create fetishists who could afford to deal in luxury bookbindings.

13.

If that picture is not a pipe, what does that picture mean?
The critic Ulises Carron: "In order to read the new art, and
to understand it, you don't need to spend five years in a
Faculty of English." But then, should we be troubled by or
grateful for *visual* illiteracy?

14.

Black and white. When we think of leaving The Book, or
even the book, to move on to the next medium, do we care who
we leave behind?

15.

Endsheet: Endsheets also may be found at beginnings.
When you come to one, turn the page.

87

Mumbo-Jumbo

A creation fable

Monday

An apotheosis of barbarism!

Come, O celestial Spirit of first reckonings, and waft me away from thy pent-up cities, sin-cursed streets and fashion-worshiping crowds, rendering at least a little service to the cause of truth; while we regret authorities, poetry and license in dealing with facts, give great animation to the ventures of day and night, and lead an easy and uncontrolled life, removed from no subject long enough to exhaust it; seduce me from the ordinary path . . . *and please begin!*

Not less refreshing were Your descriptions of tropical vegetation; the hazel-eyed nymphs, so beautiful-limbed, in their wavy motions, and in it.

Not even in the grand dignity of the quarter-deck, though You look deservingly as an impartial witness, is the veriest nonsense that ever emanated from the mudship, inside and outside, fore and aft, with living, moving, wide crowds of all pre-Paris rushing in to see and be delighted with the first monster on the Isle of Bourbon.

With Trinculo we exclaimed, "What be we here? a man or a fish?"

Sea traders, or whalers, or on any ship or ships whatever.

Biscuits, hard as gun-flints and thoroughly honeycombed.

It was in an unguarded moment that the Writer of these lines was so rash, to oblige any Editorial or other Power, ever so pen-compelled, to cool sneering wit and the perfect want of *heart* everywhere as a sort of Dominie Sampson, or mere foil to set off the Author's smartness out inhaling the breath, as in walking over the brow of a hill in summer, for example, affects us like going into the engine room of a small party, but at all times and places, we most especially admire excited chaste desire.

You, Bwana, are as fresh and vigorous as at the first line of The Book, can be transplanted to the antipodes only to bring

havoc to mountains, and the pursuit of Taurus, his wife and
child, to wit, His pleasantry, the pageantry the mirth has
been left in—if as in an allegory, the key wrought and
extravagant, is full of pictures from the "underworld," before
which he (the naturalist aforesaid) brings seven new species
of moments, generally entertaining—often ridiculous—
attaining sometimes centuries, as, pendulum-like, they swing
from island to island, each representing some fresh and novel
aspect. Great Moguls and Great Khans, Grand Lamas and
Grand Dukes, selves, sovereign Kings between worlds, creat-
ing archipelagos in the clouds—vapours reflecting from its
surface, flowers to the waters edge, a light in the brilliant
body which has attracted the public gaze and reflection:
linger and repeat the journey, verdant, unattempted yet by
prow or sailor, the reef-girt lagune-watered atoll here, there
among much that is worldly, light, fanciful and gorgeous,
that Bwana has or heard, and, if they have any significance,
are too recondite, at last, almost spoiled with the not
unfrequent sacrifice of the natural to the quaint; defects,
however Bwana is Himself—and this is saying a great deal.

Fed, lodged and entertained at the expense of the state, He
had for character, living for and by sensation, curious as an
infant, adventurous in His memory.

*—Here we pause. In our next we will pursue: infancy is
never original. In our next we will pursue comedy and
fantastic grandeur: In our next we will: pursue.*

Bwana has therefore had His eyes very wide open to the
magnificent Himself.

Tuesday

What a wild moonlight of contemplative humor bathes
that noon-day repose of allegorical fire, till, at length
nothing is left but the all-heart.

Though the mouths of dark characters are not so great, it
is then of no matter of surprise, content among the noiseless
mountains all the popularizing noise and show of his banks
of the Ohio, so far inland, which possesses a correspondent
coloring, that no new charms and mysteries remain for this

latter crow beautified with feathers of another bird; the
common sailor had never seen it before, swearing it was all
water and moonshine in a single hemisphere.

On such a slender thread hangs the whole sphere of tears,
worn, battered, warped and faded ships, cruising for months
and years in the garden of fleshy seas, a place of happy Edens
with a bursting, mirthful, Etruscan race with the flush of
powder and rivers rise most vividly overflown (so you see, to
drown the human-interest angle so that you yearn for the
world again, or for the sea).

Lunatico against all the parties.

Esteem, coupled with a most unbounded love of notoriety,
spring all those niceties of logic by which one was patron-
ized, and the other could be no possible doubt, that the prim-
itive verdict pronounced by the general practical vagueness
of these panegyrics, and the circumstances devoted by far the
greater part of His life to fortune, and everything looks
bright as a summer morning.

Bwana recovers somewhat and is diversified a little by the
"ambiguous" love (that ability) among us, and the most
provoking fact is, that in His bushels of forgiving spirit, and
who entertain the hope that the Author, seeing His bounden
critic duty of an Honest Critic to speak out the plain truth
when likely to speak, under such-and-such circumstances, be
it either truthful or fanciful; not an incoherent hodge-podge,
not worth a ship-load of honest Peter the Ambiguous, and so
He spoke.

And this is what He said:

*I, Bwana, in the midst of a long sea (wine-dark, was a son's
favorite sea) am caught and hot as a caldron. I do not particularly wish to be here, or there, with thee, but I'm here in the
midst of a long sea, not exactly gleefully, but stubbornly
poking my head into other affairs—business not entirely my
own, as if there was something to see, or say.*

And that is what He said.

Oh!

Bwana!

With the exception of a very few sentences there is scarcely
an iota of dialogue something of which is as fresh as the sea,

You spoke, an advantage of your social position, You spoke, and under pretence of some act of duty, an impossible solution when the whole world is a falsehood, an attachment of home to hide a dim stain upon Your children's memory, and the next thing He does is to commit description, the act of Isabel and Globalsphere a gloomy apparition of a house, such as it was conjured by the vague-warm effect of gloom and remote indistinctness the holy relations of the family, brother and sister, dear brother and dear sister, the stagnant pool at the bottom of power and felicity.

So rapidly and deservedly into popular favor Bwana of his proud and accomplished mother, *his sense of duty* struggles with and overcomes even the speaking Flounder who once spoke, once.

And was doomed.

And our sympathies are sought to be though not exactly with the air of Socrates pouring off his hemlock, the guy determined to live in His presence at all hazards even though a dozen outrageous in the moral sense, when he was compelled to commit infinitely worse of it to its moral tendency.

Weep we, too, with gentle Bwana; poor bud, blighted by a blow, well arranged, *du reste*—for who would not fall to the earth to hear the harmony of another tongue.

Passion can excuse incoherency, but not fine drawn mannerism, the cover of His costume, the same transcendental flights of fancy—the same abrupt starts—the once more Thou Mouldest He Anew.

Mournful, pendulous.

Upon our never-to-be-delighted-sufficiently organs of hearing; and in, serpentining melodiousness, we have found an infinite, unbounded airiness of some sanctum sanctorum, as the very best off-hand effort we could make in imitation of His healthy physical Self.

Crowds of people will run after a new pill, and swallow it with considerations of its composition quite immaterial, eat the bolus, pay the doctor himself to handle is one of no ordinary depravity; and while once an honored, now a stone.

Now shall we trace the wanting flowers and freshness of

the savannahs, but almost equally puzzling a way to get through it.

Headlong into the vasty void of the obscure, Jude the Oracular points our way with a little wholesome indignation (never more apparent than in this speculato, where legislation is the way between two shores—a rock and a hard place—a way of choosing now), so, let us legislate our ways as simply as a parrot would and be twice as comprehensible.

Wednesday

The Captain now stumps for progress as a would-be voter would, assailing his prodigious mates, as though rabbits, who try and tame the furibund sea, but all His feelings of exasperation—which even a captain feels—blow to naught against the hard-end nautical naughts of the sea blowing an intense straining at effect, bidding adieu to us; some breezes resemble Turner's later nebulous transgressions in gamboge.

Charged with dullness, our hesperian wreck of a Captain has a permanent identity of form and style, rugged and abounding picturesqueness and beauty of His scenery, like the *rat-a-tat* of the jagged mountain itself; His works sometimes have been unsatisfactory not to say ridiculous: particularly curt, not great, not remarkable, but the Captain, with one or two passages through the channel, succeeds as sensibly as would a creature with a prehensile tail, gold watch, a neglected child; He is downright good, but doings can be fundamentally bad, the Captain deals with the sea and its belongings even on dry land, but with a terrible closeness, the briefest bit of it, He died.

Stars and asterisks, or did He—no matter.

His stone: Here Lies The Briefest Bit Of Wretchedness.

From this praise we have the Bon Homme Richard and the Serapis: a battle so sanguinary and brutal in its whole character that it cannot form an attractive episode in high art; and it's to be regretted that Bwana should have dwelt so minutely upon its details not to mention, barely, Adam and

Eve's rest, so hearty and graphic that on the seventh day you'd wonder, Why rest?

To any forgotten harlot and railway wanderer, there is the sea, the glorious nebulous of which glories be.

Where with enthusiasm, and made a reputation for its Author in a day.

Thursday

Some time unable to decide whether the first of these vivid pictures, the void, was to be regarded as a mere dexterous fiction, or as a narrative of real adventurers, described in glowing, picturesque and romantic language, language one can understand; but when the later days appeared on the horizon, like a bald sun down from the hill, there could no longer exist any doubt, that although the Author was intimately acquainted with the sea of ponds, and might introduce real incidents and real characters, yet that fiction so largely entered into the composition of the earth, that they could not be regarded as intentional narratives: This has been the voice of the reader's experience.

A sailor-boy's voyage contains some pleasure and profit, thither and yon, with insane adventures amongst the natives, those beautiful metaphors, those lonely ciphers of a mistrusted imagination, the last bell and toll, the gate, the door, the moon, the sky, the plucking harp, the beatific smile, the gleaming teeth, the sonorously extravagant disguise of a rather simple-minded oafishness, all give claim to laying the reader down with a weary look—imagine how the first Reader felt, poor Bwana!—and an inward pang of regret that so much rare and lofty talent has been willfully repulsed from a theme of chance and operation, of human interest and sympathy of a high order that even the bull—with its lonely fear of tauromachy—grows fins and joins the slag of creation as it washes out to sea by an aeolian Spring gust, taking with it the mast and frigate, the rudderless fools, disembarking with all their luggage into a vast conclave of regret and earthenware with an opaque glaze of tin oxide, usually highly decorated, claim it all now in a chest of books.

Rhapsodies.

Land, full of biblical raptures, and yacht tours in the Mediterranean, seas full of exquisite description from now until the end of time.

It is a tapestry of dreams, woven with silent thread.

Call it a cloud, if you will, but seldom does land loom off the landscape and off the canvas even though it's luminous, languishing and mendacious to its every cartographer.

Unreal the scenery!

Drowsy King Media, lost in his longitudes, feels naturally rather indignant at such a tax in some way or another.

Warrent, and it will be no harm, *velut aegri somnia*, not even to the end.

A wild, furibund thing, this Bwana, who cries out for a condor's quill, driveling never but in our own eyes: bolical slang, tragi-comic bubbles as plentiful as Yankee blackberries, a thinking thing with a brow so gaunt and ribbed, so historical and evanescent that even Capt. Paul Jones plays his song on a string:

>*Oh, I wish I were in the land of cotton, oh la*
>*Land, oh la land!*

Friday

Cannot be recorded as improvements on former popular productions but rhapsodies to be added to the list is also impossible; phrases lay by the rhapsody and the raving in favor of something more temperate; to repay a perusal, rhapsody is less now than what it was; the feast of a rhapsodical noon, a summer's fest, a pleasant swoon.

In the days that this first book was read water, water was everywhere, some 70 percent of all Earth's surface called most bland, by some, who forget that land with its chiseled depths and grainy gorges is the drip of undercurrents from evapo-rated depths—falling as snow, then packing into ice, that bluey stuff gouged valleys, built glaciers and melted back to work, its self-same frozen tongue on a sprawling tip, a lemon drop.

Downstream it works its greater wonders schiesty, shiny,
sunken caves from subduction to upper mantle to a spread-
ing sea floor carrying our poor and honored and grave
Bwana around Pangaea and the West Indies and where star-
boards meet, volcanoes and quakes mark the boundaries.

Bwana cracked the Earth's crust into a dozen raft-like slabs
129 kilometers thick propelled by a molten upper mantle,
carrying landmasses like super cargoes whalers dream of:
They slipped by each other in a wrench.

Where two rafts pulled away from each other Bwana left a
rift, a great continental crust, he said, "Ahoy!", and that's
how the Atlantic Ocean grows wider by an inch each year
and that's how Bwana left a resting place in Surtsey, off the
coast of Iceland, new since 1963.

The wind often howls and sailors pray for their lives.

Kalaait Nunaat was too cold to bring settlers and tourists
so Vikings called it Greenland; lots of sailors never been
there except by washing up on its cubic shores: Eric the Red,
Henrik the Frozen Blue and some Eskimos from Ellesmere
Island, the fools.

Saturday

The Ice Age never ended here so, for the Hero of our tale,
being a warm weather owl, time to pack the paddles and
move south along the coast of Canada where cowboys on
horseback wrestle cattle in Alberta, where bush pilots fly in
supplies to polar reigns and Baffin Island whales are sunk;
still too cool; so south, so south.

Some skipper or two lost sense on the Bahamas fish-hook
islands because there are no rivers to carry silt into the sea all
these seas and spots and stars and green-blue where tuna,
marlin and galleons once sailed and Columbus first landed
in the New World on one of the 700 islands.

So now you get the drift of things; for every cabbage there
is a King.

And scenes, and all kinds of company—now floundering
with fatigue and talkative chums on their every adventure,

obliging to make them again and again, and then suddenly refreshed with a brisk sea breeze, nature's own rekindles until dawn anatomizes and speculates.

Honor and good, too, in the interval from the barber on the Mississippi boat to the Methodist minister who explains creation in his own dry way, oh reasonableness and moderation, who believes in the sword of the sea where so many sons seek to write the ode their father-in-law will understand, more beef and less thunder.

Flat as tow-paths, a voyage of 1,200 miles, generally eccentric, an inauguration of a miracle play, an orange or a peach from clime to clime over neutral tints.

One said it was the errata of creation; anyone can comment.

Sunday

Innocence suffers.

More of the same sort to come.

Whither He is going.

Come back oh come back, He was enjoined.

Release the tendency of the age He does, and to engender, we wish we were free from loss as well as Bwana but with one we must have the other; and without, without.

It wants relief, and speaks too much in the spirit of Timon; who, indeed, saw life as it is, but first wasted his money, and then shut out his heart, so that for him there was naught but naked rock: no moss, no flower.

Bwana's second, third, fourth, fifth and sixth days were remarkable and will add to His reputation.

On the seventh day He foreswore the ambition of authorship but, we trust, only for a time.

About the author

George Myers Jr. was born in 1953 in Harrisburg, Pa., and
has lived in Maine, Ohio and Kenya, East Africa. His poetry,
essays and fiction have appeared in many periodicals in
North America, Europe and Africa, including *The Quarterly,
Frank* (Paris) and *New American Writing*. He has twice been
an Ohio Arts Council Fellow (in 1986 and 1988), and has
won an Ohioana Citation for Distinguished Writing (1989),
the Governor's Award for the Arts (1988), and other awards
for his journalism and critical writing. He lives in Ohio
where he is *The Columbus Dispatch* book critic.

A note on the type

Worlds Without End was set in Baskerville Roman and
Italic by Kathryn E. King/Dual Design of Washington, D.C.
The book was printed and bound by Thomson-Shore of
Dexter, Michigan.